Forever Friends

written by Ruth Koeppel
illustrated by Cesc Mateu

Reader's Digest
Children's Books®

Pleasantville, New York • Montréal, Québec • Bath, United Kingdom

More Than Friends

A riel stood on the beach, looking down at her newly human body. Happiness! She'd never quite known the meaning of the word until now.

"Good-bye, Flounder," she tried to say, then remembered she couldn't speak. Waving good-bye instead, she headed off to find Prince Eric. Scuttle and Sebastian followed closely behind.

"We can't let her go off all by herself," declared Sebastian.

"You can hide in her room," answered Scuttle. "I'll stay close by. I've flown above Prince Eric's palace before—I know where she'll be."

Ariel rushed onward. She knew she was racing against time. *Three days to make him fall in love with me?* she thought to herself. *I can do it. I know I can!*

Suddenly, Prince Eric was there! Ariel almost fell over her new legs in surprise.

"Do I know you?" he asked, gently. "You seem familiar."

First Ariel began to nod, then she shook her head back and forth. Without her voice, communicating was confusing!

"You can't speak?" asked the Prince. "Oh, then you couldn't be who I thought…let's get you back to the palace for a change of clothes before you catch a chill."

He brought her to a beautiful guest room. "You will be my guest," he said, "until you are able to tell us your story."

A woman named Carlotta brought Ariel a dress and helped fix her hair and makeup.

Prince Eric asked his friend Grimsby to find out what was wrong with his new friend. Grimsby believed it was nothing serious. "I suggest rest and relaxation—and fun and fresh air—for this girl," he said.

Eric was happy to help Ariel. He was glad to have a distraction from his search for the girl with the perfect voice who had rescued him from the sea. He sent a note up to Ariel that promised the next day would be an adventure, filled with fun surprises.

Sebastian crept over to Ariel when the messenger left. "This is your chance to win over the Prince!" he said. Ariel was excited, but soon she collapsed on the bed, exhausted.

The next day, Carlotta arrived at dawn to help Ariel dress. Afterward, Ariel went downstairs and found Prince Eric on a beautiful white horse. He held the reins of a beautiful brown one for her to ride.

Ariel helped Sebastian into one of her saddlebags just before she and the prince headed off. Scuttle flew overhead, keeping a close eye on things.

Ariel found she was a natural-born rider—it wasn't that different from riding a dolphin. As they rode, Ariel heard waves crashing—they were heading for the beach where she had first sang to Prince Eric! Maybe being there would help him remember her.

Eric spread out a picnic blanket and the two of them had lunch while Sebastian hid behind the food, winking at Ariel as he threw her kisses and hugged himself.

After lunch, Ariel and Eric waded into the foaming surf. The Prince took Ariel's hand and walked with her along the water's edge, and told her the story of the mysterious woman who had saved him.

"It's been driving me completely crazy that I can't find her," he confided.

Ariel knew she was the one, and she was just aching to tell him. But, of course, she couldn't speak!

The sun started to set, and they rode back to the palace, where they walked hand-in-hand through a garden. They stopped by a rosebush as Sebastian and Scuttle watched. Prince Eric leaned closer to Ariel as her eyes closed and her lips puckered. "If it doesn't happen now, it never will!" squawked Scuttle.

"It'll happen," said Sebastian, "if not now, then sometime soon. Don't tell King Triton I said so, but those two are perfect together!"

Just as the prince was about to kiss Ariel, it began to rain. Eric hurried Ariel back to the palace. As she disappeared up the stairs, he called after her, "We're going for a boat ride on a lake tomorrow, so get a good-night's sleep."

Sebastian smiled. "I have some good friends in that lake," he mused. "I'll see what I can do to move this romance along. One way or another, Prince Eric is going to kiss that girl!"

Snowy Day Surprises

One winter morning, as Belle headed downstairs for breakfast, something outside caught her eye.

"Oh, look!" she cried, running over to the windows.

There had been a snowfall overnight, and the scene outside the Beast's castle was beautiful and pristine.

"Sit down and have your breakfast," Mrs. Potts told Belle.

Just then, the Beast strode into the dining room and, in her excitement, Belle practically leapt into his bowl of oatmeal.

"Look outside!" she said, bouncing up and down. "Maybe we can make some snow angels after breakfast!"

"Good morning to you, too!" the Beast said with a laugh. He understood Belle's excitement—the grounds were indeed beautiful after a new snow. Eager to impress Belle, the Beast suggested a sleigh ride to show her around.

Belle could barely eat a bite of breakfast, in spite of everyone's encouragement. Finally, Lumiere and Cogsworth gave up and went off to fetch a warm coat, hood, and gloves for Belle.

"Well, if she isn't full, at least she'll be warm," Lumiere said.

"They'll be back before I strike noon," Cogsworth chimed in.

"And wanting their tea long before teatime!" Mrs. Potts added.

The Beast and Belle headed out to the barn. Giving Phillipe a big hug hello, Belle danced around the sleigh before allowing the Beast to help her up into the seat.

"Thank you, kind sir," she said, with a smile.

Settling in beside her, the Beast took the reins and soon they were gliding through the snow.

As they drove along, Belle admired the snow on the huge trees that surrounded them. "Look at those," she said. "How beautiful they are."

"Let's stop in the field up ahead and make a snowman," the Beast suggested.

The Beast and Belle worked hard on the snowman and soon their creation was finished. The grounds began to look cheerier than they had in years.

As they climbed back into the sleigh and headed toward a field where Belle could make some snow angels, they passed some snow-covered birdhouses.

"Wait!" cried Belle. "Stop!"

The Beast guided Phillipe over to the tree. From inside the houses came scratching noises—and chirping sounds.

The holes in the houses were filled with
snow. Belle started digging, and it wasn't long
before two birds squirmed out. "They must have gotten
snowed in while they slept," said the Beast.

A third bird was trying to break the ice on the birdbath.
Belle gently broke the ice, and the
bird began to drink. As the sleigh
drove off, the birds followed
closely behind.

"Do you mind the company?"
the Beast asked, as bird wings
brushed Belle's face.

"Not at all!" she
laughed. "But their feathers
do tickle!"

She rubbed the
frozen feathers of a bird
that perched on her arm.

"Your winter wonderland is full of miracles," said Belle.

"Having you here is the miracle," the Beast answered softly.

Belle cuddled up against the Beast in the sleigh as they sped back to the castle to warm up.

When they arrived home, Belle asked Mrs. Potts for a special treat. "Can we have hot cocoa instead of tea? When I was a child, I loved having cocoa after a day out in the snow."

"I love chocolate. Let's never have tea again!" Chip said.

"Just this once, my boy!" Mrs. Potts warned him. "Teatime is for tea, and that's the way it's going to stay!"

Mrs. Potts served hot cocoa and steaming cinnamon scones, straight from the oven. Lumiere lit a fire and Cogsworth announced, "It is now tea—or rather, cocoa-time!"

Since she'd been too excited to eat breakfast, Belle wolfed down the scones and hot cocoa. Watching her, the Beast couldn't hide his pleased smile.

Belle whispered something in Mrs. Potts' ear, and it wasn't long before she came back with some oats and seeds. Phillipe poked his head in through a window and munched on the oats, while the birds gratefully ate the birdseed.

Jumping up, Belle said, suddenly, "Oh, no! I never made my snow angels."

"The snow isn't going anywhere," the Beast said. "We'll go out tomorrow and you can make as many angels as you like."

"I'd like that," Belle said, as she sat back down next to the Beast. And as the sun set, the two friends looked out the window and reflected on a wonderful day.

A Room of Her Own

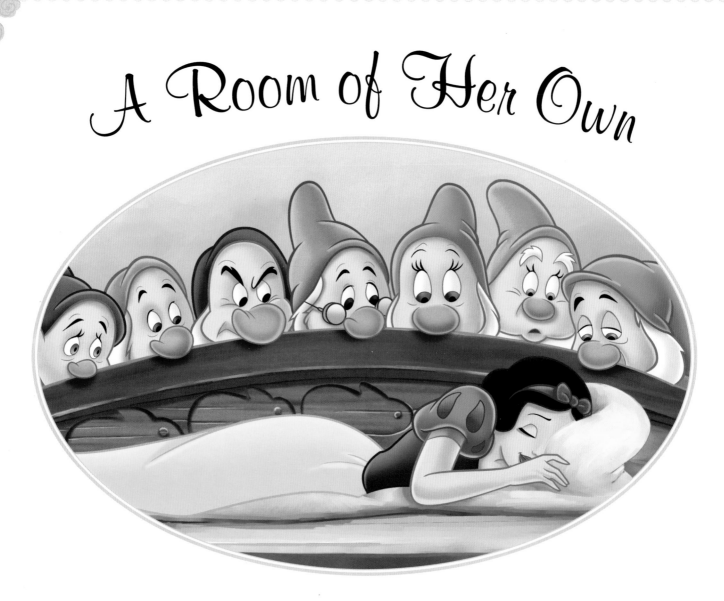

One day, the Seven Dwarfs came home from work to find Snow White cooking a wonderful dinner for them.

"You made all of our favorite foods!" cried Happy.

After they'd devoured their fabulous feast, Sleepy yawned. "I'm going to sleep well tonight," he mumbled.

"Is it bedtime already? Is Snow White using our room again?" groaned Grumpy. "I'm tired of sleeping on the floor!"

"It *is* uncomfortable," agreed Sleepy, with a yawn. "But nothing stops me from catching forty winks."

The Dwarfs looked over at their guest—she'd fallen asleep on the couch!

"Cooking that big meal tired her out," said Doc. "Hey, I know how we can stay in our room! We can build Snow White a new room—in the attic!"

The Dwarfs got to work. They made four bedposts out of four trees. The beavers and woodpeckers helped Bashful carve forest animals on the headboard, and Doc made beautiful leaves and flowers. Then, Happy finished the headboard with lots of beautiful jewels.

Next, they built a wardrobe for Snow White's clothes. The squirrels brought in pinecones so Doc could make a lamp for the bedside table. At first, the Dwarfs carpeted the floor with soft needles from a white pine tree. But somehow that didn't seem right—Snow White deserved the very best! So they finished a rug they'd been weaving for their living room. There was plenty of time before winter to make another for themselves.

The birds provided feathers for Snow White's mattress. And the rabbits gave some fur for a pillow.

"Achoo!" burst out Sneezy. "Watch where you put that stuff!"

Doc and Dopey sewed silk squares into a beautiful quilt—and the birds laid a canopy on top of the four posts.

Almost done! The final touch was a staircase that reached from the second floor all the way up to the attic, so Snow White could climb up and down easily.

The Dwarfs were very proud of their work. They liked it so much, they wanted to move in themselves.

"If I slept in the attic bedroom, I could take a break from the rest of you when I'm in a bad mood!" said Grumpy.

The Dwarfs heard Snow White get up from her chair. Startled, they ran downstairs to greet her.

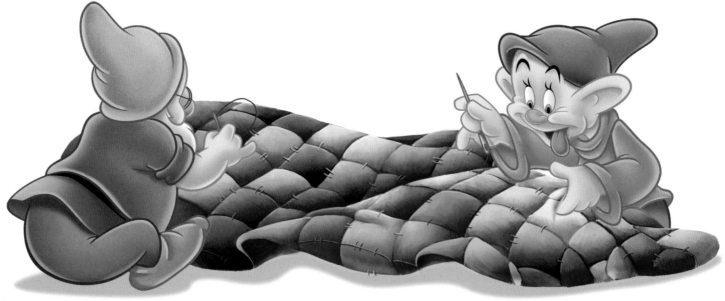

"What have you been up to?" she asked, as she slowly climbed the spiral staircase. "Oh, my goodness!" she burst out. Then, she started to cry.

"Oh, no, she doesn't like it!" said Bashful, and he started to cry, too.

Snow White gave him a big hug. "No, I love it! I can't believe you made this all for me!"

The Dwarfs hopped around the room, pointing things out and showing off their work.

The friends all settled down as Snow White told the Dwarfs a story. "Someday, I will be a princess and live in a palace," she told them. "And there will be seven bedrooms where you can stay when you come to visit."

"For once in our lives, we'll each have a little privacy!" Grumpy said. Snow White and the Dwarfs laughed.

"Wait," said Snow White. "Where is Sleepy?"

The Dwarfs searched the room, peering into corners and looking under things. Then Dopey pulled back the covers of Snow White's quilt—Sleepy had fallen asleep in the new bed!

"Wake up, Sleepy," cried Doc. "It's time for breakfast!"

"That's right," said Snow White. "Go wash up and get ready for the best breakfast ever. You must be hungry from all that hard work!"

Moving Day

The day Cinderella moved into the palace she brought almost nothing from her old life with her. Well, nothing except for a few old dresses, portraits of her parents, and some very special friends. Cinderella's dog Bruno, and her mouse friends Gus, Jaq, and Mary were right by her side.

After a long journey to the palace, she finally arrived. The palace staff was lined up in full-dress uniform. Standing at the head of the line was Prudence, the first lady-in-waiting. Looking Cinderella up and down, she forced a smile.

"I'm Prudence," she said, with a curtsy. "Welcome, Your Highness. We're delighted to hear about the wedding."

"Thank you," said Cinderella, shyly. She knew she shouldn't be intimidated by Prudence, but frankly—she was!

Cinderella realized that the rest of the staff were all whispering about her clothing. And she'd worn her best dress.

Prudence brought Cinderella to a beautiful room. The wardrobe was full of dresses—made especially for her! There was also a shiny new brush and comb on her dressing table.

After Prudence left, Cinderella and the mice went looking for Bruno. When they'd arrived earlier, the gamekeeper took Bruno to tour the kennels where the other hounds stayed. But the gamekeeper wasn't sure what to make of a common, undignified dog like Bruno.

"He's not much of a hunter, Miss, he's really more of a…pet," the man said. "Perhaps it's best if he stays with you."

"Of course!" Cinderella cried, hugging Bruno and taking him away from the kennel. The friends all headed back to the palace and, exhausted from their long day, fell asleep.

At the crack of dawn, a voice interrupted Cinderella's dreams. "*Ahem.* Good morning, Your Highness! I'm Daphne."

Daphne was about to place a breakfast tray on the bed, when she noticed the mice all over Cinderella's pillows. She screamed and spilled the tray. Worst of all, the list of Cinderella's daily activities fell into the mess, too. Daphne ran to fetch Prudence.

Prudence frowned at the mess. "Why do you have an entourage of mice—instead of a proper staff? We are trying to rid the palace of mice, not bring more in!"

A loud *meow* came from behind Prudence, and a white cat peeked around her legs.

Prudence bent down to pet her. "This was Pom-Pom's room before you arrived," she said. "Why don't you two get to know each other?" she called over her shoulder, as she left the room.

Pom-Pom sniffed the air. Then, she turned to Bruno and hissed. Bruno growled. The mice cowered behind Cinderella.

"Okay, everyone," Cinderella said. "This is a big palace and we don't have to get in each other's way. But it would be nice if we could all try to get along. Please? For me?"

Bruno backed down, and licked Cinderella's hand. Cinderella brushed Pom-Pom's hair, and the mice tied on some new ribbons!

Prudence returned and gave Cinderella a new schedule. "This is to replace the one that got ruined!" she said.

Cinderella sighed. "I know that I'll have a lot to do as a princess. But I need time for myself, too. Do you think that could be arranged?" she asked.

"Princesses have lots of royal duties," Prudence answered. "All the other princesses I've known have had full schedules."

"I know," said Cinderella, thoughtfully. "But if I were like all the other princesses, the prince wouldn't have wanted me to be *his* Princess!"

"All right," Prudence said. "We'll work on your schedule."

"Cinderelly," said Mary, "I think we mice would get along better with the ladies if we had duties, too."

Cinderella thought for a moment. Mary was right—if her friends were going to get along with everyone, they would have to work in the palace.

"Gus-Gus would be good footman!" offered Gus.

Jaq smiled, "I'd like a fancy new uniform."

The Prince came home that evening, happy to find
Cinderella settled in so well. At dinner that night, Cinderella
and the Prince commented on the beautiful table decorations
that Mary made. Gus and Jaq stood by proudly as the couple
dined. And Cinderella and the Prince toasted each other, and
the beginning of their new life together.